KU-448-580

One day Zippy is trying out some card tricks when George says he can do real magic. Can The Great Georgio really make Bungle disappear?

# rainbow

## THE MAGIC
## SHOW

Written by Mike Butcher
Illustrated by David Brian

Copyright © 1991 Thames Television Plc.
All rights reserved.
Published in Great Britain by World International Publishing Limited,
An Egmont Company, Egmont House PO Box 111,
Great Ducie Street, Manchester M60 3BL.
Printed in Germany. ISBN 0 7498 0321 5
REPRINTED 1993

*A CIP catalogue record for this book is available from the British Library*

"Pick a card, George!" says Zippy.
"Take a look at it, but don't let me see
what it is." Zippy is trying to play a card
trick on his friend.

George takes a card and has a good look at it.

"Now I will use my special magical powers to guess what your card is," Zippy tells him.

Zippy closes his eyes and thinks very hard.

"Er . . . is your card the Ace of Hearts?" he asks George.

"Yes!" gasps George. "That's amazing, Zippy!"

"It's easy when you have special magical powers like me," boasts Zippy.
Bungle has been watching Zippy doing his card trick.

"Can I have a go, too, Zippy?" asks Bungle. "Let me pick a card." Bungle reaches out to take a card, but he knocks them all out of Zippy's hand!

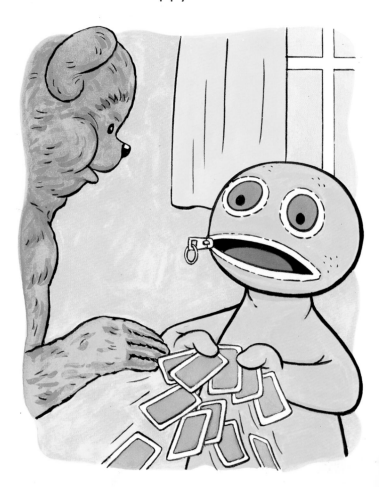

Zippy drops all the cards on the floor.
Bungle and George both see that every
card is the Ace of Hearts!

"Oh, what a cheat you are, Zippy!"
says George.

"I thought you had special magical powers, Zippy!" Bungle grins, helping him pick up all the cards.

"Er, well . . . I have," insists Zippy. "I must have changed all these cards into the Ace of Hearts by magic." Bungle and George don't believe him at all!

"I can do real magic," George tells his friends.

"Don't be silly, George!" scoffs Zippy.
"You can't do real magic. There's no such
thing! I was only pretending, so I could
trick you!"

George decides to prove that he can do magic by putting on a special magic show. He is going to dress up as the famous magician . . . The Great Georgio!

When George goes to get changed for his show, Zippy starts to feel hungry.

"I'll just find something to eat in the kitchen while we're waiting," he tells Bungle.

Zippy goes out to the kitchen and has a look around. He soon finds a packet of biscuits.

"These look tasty," he smiles, licking his lips.

By the time Zippy comes back with the biscuits, The Great Georgio is almost ready to start his show. Zippy has to hurry up and sit down!

"For my first trick, I will need a
volunteer from the audience," announces
The Great Georgio.

"I'll help you," says Bungle, standing
up.

"Thank you, Bungle," says Georgio. "Now I will make you disappear!"

"You'll never make Bungle-Bonce disappear!" laughs Zippy. "He's much too big!"

The Great Georgio waves a sheet in front of Bungle and says a few magic words.

"What a silly trick," chuckles Zippy as he watches.

Zippy is very surprised to see that, when Georgio drops the sheet, Bungle really has disappeared!

"Where has he gone?" Zippy gasps.

"I've made him disappear with my magic, Zippy," smiles Georgio. "I told you I could do it, didn't I?" Zippy can hardly believe his eyes!

Just then, Zippy hears a loud sneeze
from behind the sofa.

"What was that noise?" Zippy
wonders, going round to have a look for
himself.

Zippy finds Bungle hiding behind the sofa!

"So The Great Georgio didn't make you disappear at all!" says Zippy. "You were just hiding from me!"

"I'm sorry about that, Georgio!" says Bungle, standing up. "It's a little bit dusty behind the sofa, where you told me to hide. It made me sneeze!"

"I suppose you are right, Zippy," sighs Georgio. "I can't really make things disappear."

"No, but I can!" grins Zippy. "Just you watch this!"

Zippy races over to where he was
sitting and picks up his packet of biscuits.
His friends can't understand what he is up
to.

"Now I'll show you some real magic. Watch me make these biscuits disappear!" Zippy laughs, starting to eat them. Bungle and George can't help laughing, too!